With love to my sisters and brothers
Thomas and Deborah Niehof
Daniel and LuAnn Kruis
Beth Walburg
Timothy and Marcelle Walburg

In memory of my great aunts
Mae and Nell Goudzwaard
I can't wait to see you again

—L.W.

To my mother, Barbara Bernardin,
Who first shared the story with me

—J.B.

The Legend of the

EASTER EGG

by Lori Walburg

Illustrated by
James Bernardin

Zonderkidz™
The Children's Group of ZondervanPublishingHouse

One April morning when the air was soft and sweet, a boy and his sister went outside to gather eggs.

"Easter's coming," the sister said. "Let's pretend we're hunting Easter eggs."

"What are Easter eggs?" the boy asked.

"Don't you remember?" the girl said.

He thought and thought, but he couldn't remember. He was going to ask again, but just then, she scared up a hen, squawking, from its nest in the grass. "Look!" she cried. Smiling, she held up a rosy brown egg.

That night, the boy woke to the sound of his name. "Thomas!" His mother's face bent over his. "Your sister is sick. Papa must take you away."

Thomas let his mother slip off his warm nightshirt. He held up his arms as she pulled a sweater over his head, and sat down when she tugged on his knickers. When she told him he could not see Lucy, he nodded. When Papa told him where he was taking him, he smiled.

But he was not really awake. He did not understand.

When he woke again, Thomas did not know where he was. His bedroom was gone. Mama, Papa, and Lucy were gone. But before he could even think about being scared, his eyes grew wide and he sat bolt upright.

Had he died? Was this heaven? Because all around him was candy. Long branches of licorice and tiny jeweled rock candy. Yellow, white, purple, and pink jellybeans. Marshmallow chicks and tiny chocolate eggs. He stood up very slowly.

"Morning, Thomas!" a familiar voice said.

It was John Sonneman. Thomas had come to stay with John and his new wife, Mary, at their candy store. Just as Papa had said.

All that long Wednesday, Thomas helped Mr. Sonneman in his store. He filled jars of candy. He weighed chocolate on the tippy scales and scrubbed the counter till it gleamed. All day, Mr. Sonneman let him eat smidgens of fudge and bits of broken peppermint sticks.

When he finished cleaning out the cookstove for Mrs. Sonneman, she looked at him and laughed. "Goodness, gracious!" she said. "You have ash on your face!"

With her thumb, she wiped him clean. He smiled. But inside, his heart felt as dusty and grey as the ash. His sister was sick. He couldn't be with her. And there was nothing he could do.

On Sunday after church, Thomas went outside to play. At the edge of a small stream, he broke off a young reed, put it between his two thumbs, and blew. "Squawk!"

"Ok-a-lay!" a red-winged blackbird sang in reply. Two swallows whirled overhead. "Cheer! Cheer!" they cried.

Suddenly, Thomas threw the reed at them, then snatched up pebbles and threw them too. A robin cocked his head, peering at him with one eye. "Tut-tut," it chided.

"Silly birds," Thomas muttered as he turned away.

More days passed. Thomas learned that Lucy had scarlet fever. A red rash covered her body. Her face burned with fever. Every night at dinner, John Sonneman prayed for her to get well.

Sometimes, Mary Sonneman felt his forehead. He wished he could be sick too. But his body was white and healthy. And his face, cool and dry.

On Thursday, Mary sent him out to trade for eggs. When he returned, his shoes and socks were caked in mud.

"Spring!" Mary laughed. "So beautiful and so messy at the same time." Kneeling, she took off his shoes and socks, then cleaned his feet in a pail of warm water. The water tickled his toes, and for the first time in days, he giggled.

Friday dawned bleak and cold. At noon, the stores closed. And everyone went to church.

Thomas listened to the story of Jesus' death. The minister talked for a long time. "Though your sins be as scarlet, they shall be as white as snow," he said.

While the adults shared bread and wine, Thomas slowly ate a white peppermint. Then he ate a pink peppermint. For a while, he forgot Lucy. Snuggled under John Sonneman's arm, he fell asleep.

He awoke to bedlam. Lanterns and candles flashed against the dark afternoon. Overhead, something terrible battered at the roof of the church. Thomas gripped John Sonneman's hand as the townspeople crowded at the doorway, peering out.

"Hail," they said.

High above, the church bell swung wildly, pelted by icy pebbles. As the afternoon passed and the hail turned to freezing rain, the bell fell silent. Frozen.

That night, as Mary Sonneman tucked him into bed, Thomas asked, "Is Lucy going to die, just like Jesus did?"

"Shh," said Mary. "She will not die. She is just very sick."

"I want to see her!" he cried. "I want to be with her!"

"Soon," Mary said. "She is almost well. You will see her soon."

She put her hand into her pocket and pulled out a small chocolate egg. "Here is your first Easter egg," she said. "Sunday is Easter. On Easter, you will see your sister again."

Thomas remembered hunting for eggs. And he remembered the question that Lucy had never answered. "What are Easter eggs?" he asked again.

She pressed the small egg into his palm and wrapped his fingers around it. "Three days after Jesus died, early on Sunday morning, some women came to Jesus' tomb," she said. "They were sad. They had come to mourn Jesus' death. But when they arrived, they saw the stone had been rolled away from the tomb!"

Thomas held up the egg. "Did the stone look like this?"

Mary laughed. "Yes, only much bigger and much heavier!"

Mary continued, "Then an angel came and told the women that Jesus was not there. He was alive! Filled with joy and fear, the women ran to tell the other disciples. And that was the first Easter."

"But why do we have Easter eggs?" Thomas asked.

Mary explained, "Just as a chick breaks out of an egg, so had Jesus broken free of the tomb of death. Easter eggs remind us that Jesus conquered death and gives us eternal life."

"So Lucy won't die?"

Mary shook her head. "Someday she will. And you will too. But if you believe in Jesus, you will see each other again in heaven. That is the promise and joy of Easter!"

She tucked the blanket under his chin. "Remember," she said, "believe in Jesus. Hope and pray. That's what you can do for your sister. All right?"

"Okay," Thomas agreed.

All day Saturday, Thomas stayed inside and colored eggs. Outside, the freezing rain fell. But inside, he stood near the glowing cookstove, dipping eggs. As he plunged the cool white eggs into the warm red dye, he thought of Lucy's fever. He remembered the story of the Easter egg. And for the first time in his life, he prayed. All by himself.

Very early Easter morning, before anyone woke up, Thomas filled a basket with colored eggs and slipped out the door. As he walked, the sun came up. And all around him, the world began to sparkle.

The twigs on the trees and the tiny buds sparkled. The stubbled wheat fields and the long, waving reeds sparkled. Even the icebent daffodils and crushed violets, the trampled crocuses and the battered hyacinths glittered like jewels in the muddy farmyards. Thomas caught his breath. He had never seen anything so beautiful.

He passed the cemetery. The gravestones, too, twinkled in their shining gowns of ice.

And the church bell began to ring.

When he got home, Thomas bounded up the stairs to Lucy's room. Finally, he would see her. Finally, he would tell her. Of the story of the Easter egg. Of his faith in Jesus. His hope for new life. And the love they shared that would never, ever, end.

Traditions and Symbols of Lent and Easter

The forty days before Easter are traditionally known as Lent. Lent begins on Ash Wednesday. In the Old Testament, God's people put ashes on themselves when they were deeply sorry for their sins. On Ash Wednesday, Christians receive the mark of ashes on their foreheads to remind them of their sins and their need to repent.

On Maundy Thursday, Christians remember Jesus' Last Supper with his disciples. They break bread, to remind them of Christ's broken body. And they drink wine, to remind them of Christ's shed blood. Sometimes, they will wash each other's feet, to remind them to serve and love each other, as Christ loved his disciples and served them by washing their feet.

On Good Friday, Christians remember Christ's death. Through Scripture readings, sermons, prayers, and hymns, they worship Jesus and commemorate his suffering and death.

Finally, on Easter Sunday, Christians celebrate Christ's resurrection. The egg, an ancient symbol of new life, has become for Christians a symbol of the resurrection. Through the gift of Easter eggs, Christians remind each other that through Christ's resurrection, they too will conquer death and receive the gift of eternal life.

❦

The Legend of the Easter Egg. Text copyright © 1999 by Lori Walburg. Illustrations copyright © 1999 by James Bernardin.

Walburg, Lori. The legend of the Easter egg / by Lori Walburg ; illustrated by James Bernardin.   p.   cm.
Summary: While preparing for Easter in his small prairie town, Thomas hears the story of the resurrection of Jesus and discovers the meaning of new life through the symbolism of the Easter egg. Includes information page about the traditions and symbols of Lent and Easter. ISBN 0-310-22447-0 (jacketed caseside) 0-310-22741-0 (printed caseside) [1. Easter eggs—Fiction.   2. Easter—Fiction.   3. Jesus Christ—Resurrection—Fiction.   4. Christian life—Fiction.]   I. Bernardin, James, ill.   II. Title.
PZ7.W1337Le   1999 [E]—dc21 98-47180 CIP AC

This edition printed on acid-free paper and meets the American National Standards Institute Z39.48 standard.

All rights reserved. Requests for information should be addressed to Zondervan Publishing House, Grand Rapids, MI 49530.
Printed in China. 99 00 01 02 03 04/ ❖ HK/ 10 9 8 7 6 5 4 3

The illustrations in this book were done in acrylic and colored pencil on paper.

With humble thanks to Kathy Bieber, for providing the initial research
on Easter eggs, and with deep gratitude to Bob Hudson, Shelley Townsend-Hudson,
and Susan Hill, my first and best readers. —L.W.